Baby

YO-CCL-809

Written by Catherine McCafferty
Illustrated by Erin Mauterer
Cover illustrated by Mitch Hyatt

Louis Weber, C.E.O., Publications International, Ltd.
7373 North Cicero Avenue, Lincolnwood, Illinois 60712
Ground Floor, 59 Gloucester Place, London W1U 8JJ

Customer Service: 1-800-595-8484 or customer_service@pilbooks.com

www.pilbooks.com

p i kids is a trademark of Publications International, Ltd., and is registered in the United States.

8 7 6 5 4 3 2 1

Manufactured in China.

ISBN-13: 978-0-7853-1926-9
ISBN-10: 0-7853-1926-3

Clover loved to munch grass in her spot by the split gray rock. The grass there was so good that Clover thought it must be the sweetest grass in the whole field.

Then Clover saw Daisy eating grass near a patch of flowers. Daisy looked so happy that Clover thought she'd try the grass over there.

Clover pushed Daisy out of the way and ate the grass. Clover thought this grass tasted even sweeter than the grass by the split gray rock.

Clover was happy in her new spot until she saw her sister Lily eating the grass by the fence. Lily's grass looked so good that Clover thought she would try it.

Daisy and Lily were angry. "What's wrong?" asked Sweetheart, the wisest cow in the field.

"Clover pushed me and then ate the grass in my spot," said Daisy.

"She did the same thing to me," said Lily.

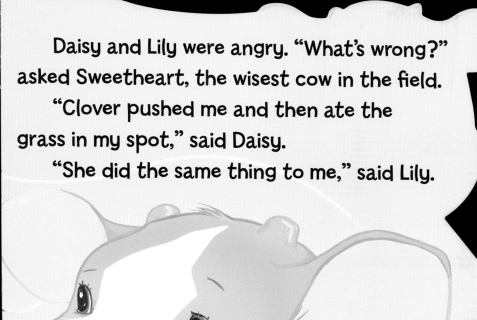

Sweetheart knew just what to do. She went to Clover and asked, "Would you like to taste the sweetest grass in the whole field?"

"Of course," said Clover.

"Well close your eyes, and I'll take you to it."

Clover closed her eyes while Sweetheart led her across the field. With her eyes still closed, Clover started to eat. "Yum!" she said, "this grass really is the best."

When Clover opened her eyes, she saw the split gray rock. She was right back where she had started! From then on, Clover was happy in her own spot.